For the one and only Miles George Shirreffs,
love from Great Auntie Jeannie x – J.W.

For Toosy (Lucy), my very first friend – J.D.

tiger tales
5 River Road, Suite 128, Wilton, CT 06897
Published in the United States 2015
Originally published in Great Britain 2015
by Little Tiger Press
Text copyright © 2015 Jeanne Willis
Illustrations copyright © 2015 Jenni Desmond
ISBN-13: 978-1-58925-169-4
ISBN-10: 1-58925-169-5
Printed in China
LTP/1800/0993/0914
10 9 8 7 6 5 4 3 2 1

For more insight and activities, visit us at www.tigertalesbooks.com

THE FIRST SLODGE

WIIHUHAWN

yawn

scratch
scratch

by
JEANNE WILLIS · illustrated by JENNI DESMOND

tiger tales

Once upon a slime, there was a Slodge.
The first Slodge in the universe.

She saw the first sunrise.

And the first sunset.

"My day, my night," she said.

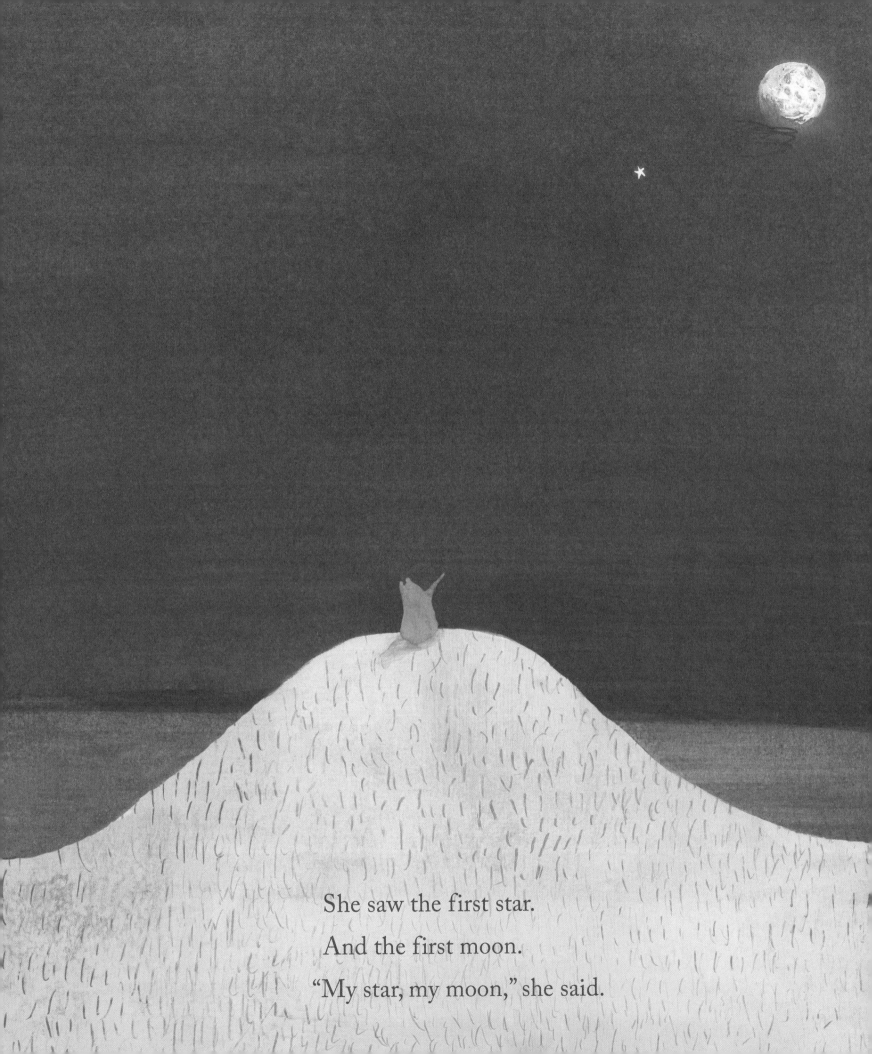

She saw the first star.
And the first moon.
"My star, my moon," she said.

She heard the first thunder,
and saw the first lightning.

She smelled the first flower . . .

and picked the first fruit.
"Mine, all mine!" she said.

She took a bite of the fruit,
then went to sleep.
As she slept, she dreamed
she was hungry.

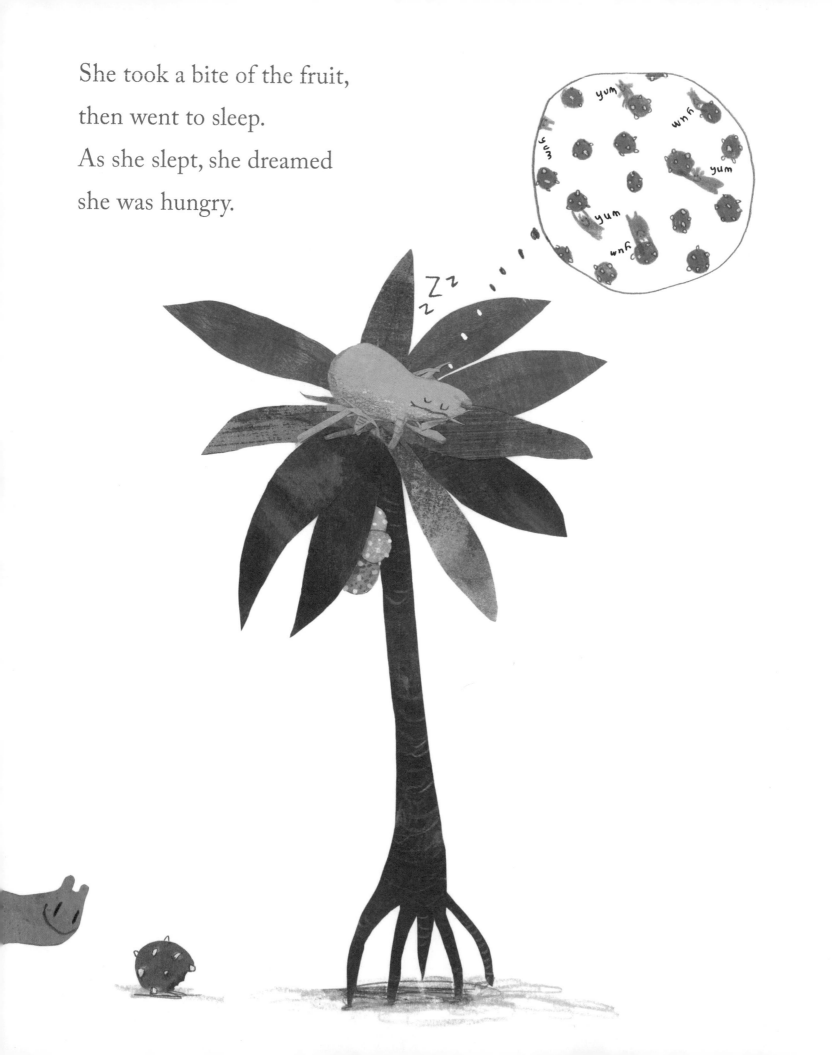

She woke up and went to eat the fruit.
But somebody had taken a second bite.

There was another Slodge!

It was a huge shock to both of them.

Each thought it was the only one.

"My fruit!" said the First Slodge.

"*My* fruit!" said the Second.

And they fought the first fight.

The fruit rolled down the hill.

"Mine!" they said as they ran to catch it.

The fruit fell into the sea.

The First Slodge jumped in after it.

"My sea!" said the First Snawk.

"My Slodge, my supper!"

And it went to eat her.

The Second Slodge was furious.

"That's *my* Slodge!" he said.

He jumped in with a splash . . .

scared away the Snawk, and saved her.

"You are my friend," said the First Slodge.

"No, you are *my* friend," said the Second.

And they shared the fruit and the friendship.

The sun went down.

"Our sunset," said the First Slodge.

"Our moon, our stars," said the Second.

The world didn't belong to anyone.

It belonged to *everyone*.

It was there to share.

Once upon a slime, there were two Slodges.

But not for long . . . .

"*Our* babies!"